I0746294

Copyright 2024, Steve Davala
www.stevedavala.com
Story by Laurie and Steve Davala
Artwork by Francesca Da Sacco
ISBN: 978-1-7370984-9-2
All Rights Reserved

The Books Bit Me Back!

Story by Laurie and Steve Davala
Art by Francesca Da Sacco

Did you read the first book?
In case you missed it, go read
'Books are for Reading, Not Eating!'
also by Steve and Laurie Davala, and
illustrated by Francesca Da Sacco.
It's a story about a little girl
who eats books and turns into
whatever the book is about!

Maybe now you can see why
'The Books Bit Me Back!'

UNDER the SEA
THE KITE
CARS
THE ELF

Remember our friend Liz Mckeeting?
Who used to eat books meant for reading?
Though she stopped eating stories,
Poems or allegories,
Her books were still scared of her feeding.

MATH
2·4÷
6+7
2-4

The pages all texted in fear.
"What will happen when her mother's
not here?
Will *Liz* eat our pages
at once or in stages?
It's time we snap into high gear."

the SWORD in the STONE

They waited 'til Liz got in bed,
on her nightstand, some books she'd
just read.
"We won't let her dine.
Let's show her some spine.
And this time we'll eat her instead!"

"What's that?" Liz stared at the stack.
"Could it be that the books bit me back?!
The more that I look,
It seems I've entered a book
These stories have made me their snack!"

In a house with three bowls, beds,
and chairs,
Her hunger overpowered her cares.
An odor arose,
And she scrunched up her nose,
And from the window
she saw three bear stares.

"It's over, the bears are now here!"
"For certain she'll soon disappear!"
But by the book's end,
Baby bear made a friend,
And Liz ate a fourth mush with a cheer.

"Alas! What a smart little girl."
Said the next book, "Let me take a whirl."
When Liz said goodnight,
With a gigantic bite,
The book chomped on a little red curl.

Liz awoke in a dark shadow land.
The book said, "This will be grand!"
Yet Liz walked about,
not the slightest of doubt,
despite what the merry book planned.

Some thieves slunk, up to no good.
But they were just misunderstood.
Liz grabbed a small bow,
Put on a big show,
And said "I'll be your new Robin Hood!"

This put the books into a rage.
Worried she'd eat one more page.
A book cackled with glee
"She'll be eaten by me,
And we'll bring her to a dark Middle Age."

ARTHUR'S YOUTH WAS
A TIME WHEN HE WAS
TUTORED BY MERLYN TO
PREPARE HIM FOR THE USE
OF POWER AND ROYAL LIFE.
THE SETTING IS LOOSELY BASED
ON MEDIEVAL ENGLAND.

Liz stood there all on her own.
But look how the little girl's grown.
The kingdom bowed down,
They brought her a crown,
As Liz pulled a sword from a stone.

The books all lined up to surrender.
Not a thing they could think of would end her.
"She'll eat us, it's true,
But there's nothing to do,
Will she cook us or opt for a blender?"

ATION

"Don't worry dear books, I won't dine,
I love getting lost in a line,
I love your tales every minute,
When I'm entirely stuck in it,
Shall I wear ketchup or is mustard just fine?"

TREES & PLANTS
A RED BALLOON
the GIFT
ON VACATION
the SWORD in the STONE
ROBIN HOOD
the
END

www.ingramcontent.com/pod-product-compliance
Lightning Source LLC
Chambersburg PA
CBHW080911190726
48294CB00008B/2050